Joseph Turnley

Reveries of Affection

In Memory of that good and beloved Princ, his Royal Highness the late

Prince consort, who departed this life on the fourteenth day of December

1861

Joseph Turnley

Reveries of Affection
In Memory of that good and beloved Princ, his Royal Highness the late Prince consort, who departed this life on the fourteenth day of December 1861

ISBN/EAN: 9783337172367

Printed in Europe, USA, Canada, Australia, Japan

Cover: Foto ©Raphael Reischuk / pixelio.de

More available books at **www.hansebooks.com**

REVERIES OF AFFECTION

IN MEMORY OF.

THAT GOOD AND BELOVED PRINCE

His Royal Highness the late Prince Consort

WHO DEPARTED THIS LIFE

ON THE

FOURTEENTH DAY OF DECEMBER 1861

" The righteous never die "

It is not intended to publish this book, the circulation of which will be a few complimentary copies to friends and certain distinguished persons, especially of that profession of which the Author is a very humble member.

Rochfort Tower,

South Norwood, Surrey.

1868.

OSBORNE, *February* 27, 1868.

SIR,

I received this morning from the gentleman to whom you entrusted it, the book which you desire to present to Her Majesty, and had the honour of placing it in Her Majesty's hands.

The Queen desires me to express her thanks to you for your attention in causing so beautiful a work to be prepared for her acceptance.

I have the honour to be,

SIR,

Your obedient humble servant,

T. H. BIDDULPH.

J. TURNLEY, ESQ.

THE MEMORIALS OF DEPARTED WORTH

REVIVE THE LIFE OF VIRTUE AND GOODNESS,

AND OFT REALIZE

THOSE SWEET REVERIES

OF WHICH THE ARDENT AND FAITHFUL PARTAKE,

AS PART OF THE

PRIVILEGES AND SORROWS OF

UNCHANGING LOVE.

SUCH THOUGHTS MAY PLEAD FOR THIS

TRIBUTE TO "THE GOOD"

BY

IMMERITUS.

First Reverie.

PROVERBS xiv. 10.

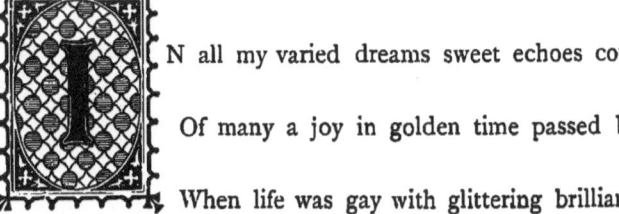 N all my varied dreams sweet echoes come

Of many a joy in golden time passed by,

When life was gay with glittering brilliancy,

When hopes were mine as bright as Summer's stars,

When every day some pleasing circumstance

Enshrined sweet constant love. I deemed not then

How soon the solace of this throbbing heart

Would be poor Memory's vivid portraiture,

On which Love lives until that solemn day

When my dear treasure shall be mine again,

Though ta'en away so suddenly—now gone

(Oh, what is buried in those words "now gone!")

To that supernal world where angels dwell,

And where each weary one serenely rests.

Yet may we weep for all the good and just,

For those who sleep awhile in silent death.

Ah, yes! there is a melody in woe,

Which lives a consecrated life alone;

Its gentle spirit lulls the human heart,

Until the storms of Time have passed away;

Though ever and anon come rolling tears,

Which in their course oft find some hidden wound;

And murmuring sighs—the soft, long-lasting sighs:

For these there are no words or characters;

No earthly power may dare to stay their course,

For they proceed from God's great dwelling-place.

Take me, then, Grief, and teach my anxious heart,

Divorced from all save Memory and Heaven,

To join with thee in close companionship;

For thou hast fashion fair and comeliness,

And ever tenderest thy best address,

To stay my fears and hold the place of Love—

My precious friend, as Love was wont to be.

And, when I start at shadows of the night,

Or dream of happiness in scenes of youth,

Thy sweet enchanting tongue will tell of joys

To come, and of my everlasting life.

Then who shall raise the veil which hides the tear,

Fresh from the haven of my broken heart?

There was a day when Love's first star appeared:

E'en from its holy secrecy it came;

Glowing with light from the eternal world,

To gladden Time with its fair beauteousness.

With trembling lips the tale of joy was told,

A sacred bond unseen by mortal eyes

Was sealed, and lies amongst the things of truth,

In the great archives of Eternity,

To await the revelations of all Time.

Yes, once, and only once, I loved—sweet trance !

As first the glance of new-born infant peers

And feels the light of Heaven—what mystic thrill

(All ecstacy !) attends that rushing beam !

'Tis even thus with precious Love's first throb ;

In noble hearts 't is indefinable.

All-joyous peace !—it gave a zest to life,

That until then had been but dreary oft.

There was a time, I thought how bright and safe

My destiny—how loved and sure my home—

How well entrenched from every incident

Which could defeat or lessen our delight!

But shadows fell upon our happiness,

And then a missive Angel suddenly

Appeared, involved within a heavy cloud,

Unloosed our bands, and took my Love to Heaven.

Since then hours lag like idle schoolboys' steps:

Yet I would check these tears; in love I would.

But, when I think of that endearing one,

And of his gentleness, once all my own,

(Who for his graciousness was ta'en to Heaven,)

I ask kind intercession for these sighs.

Oh, there are thoughts within the sorrowing mind

Beyond the utterance of the stammering tongue,

Which may not in this joyous world be heard.

Yet in bright Summer's happy radiance

Come bold tornadoes, led by Eurus' hand;

And then may man not start to see Hope's flowers

All scattered rudely by the boist'rous winds—

His herds dispersed, affrighted in dismay;

His home by maddening storms rent all in twain,

And those he loved deep swallowed in the gulf!

Of all bereft, he wanders to and fro,

To seek some lonely spot from common ken;

Deep sighs succeed each other plaintingly;

No loved one then to stay the falling tear,

Or chide with sweet Affection's gentle word.

Say, can I e'er forget that tenderness—

Those ready sacrifices amply made—

That truthfulness when first Affection's eye

Encountered mine with frank and genial glance?

Yes, that assuring voice, so fond, sincere,

Soon banished all the clouds of my young life,

And lit it up with beatific joys.

Since then my heart-strings intertwined with thine,

And they must break ere I can yield thee up.

For me, thy country and sweet childhood's home,

And all the kindred of thy peerless life,

The loved associates of thy youthful days,—

All these and more were quickly counted nought

In that dear moment when I called thee mine :

O'er these and thee my memory ever dwells.

Rebuke not, Love! I would be just to all;

Yet I would draw on Memory's vast store

Loved images of thee, so lately mine.

Yes, yes, I see thee now! thy kind and glowing eye,

Floating in tenderness, upon me beams;

A smile yet wanders o'er that noble brow,

Enthroned with manly purposes serene,

Arrayed with grace and in perfection clad.

Bewitching dream! yes, all was brilliant then;

As light from Angels' eyes my life was bright!

Dear, ever dear, was then our happy home!

Alas! how soon and oft come Fortune's ills!

Just as the Morn goes forth in sandals grey,

And the gawd Sun hath set the hills on fire,

And sweetest airs come rushing through the vales,

(Rousing young Echo from her fairy lair,)

Breathing new life in Nature's loveliness,—

The random shot reverberates aloud!

Frights the young deer then nestling in her home.

The heedless sportsman pauses not to watch

The crested eagle riven from her mate :

She hastes and veers from peak to haughty height,

Then tries the well-known fissures of the rocks,

Amidst the lofty clouds and threatening storms.

Through all the wilderness of winds she flies,

Looks on a kingdom desert now of love,

Soars with the rising gale, and veers away

Where late in sport they tarried many an eve ;

Yet nought but Echo answers her shrill cry.

The avalanche, as heard in other days,

Roars loud and crumbles in the vale below;

The swift chamois comes bounding near her nest,—

She scarce essays to note the intrusive step,

For joy and peace no more illume her home.

Distraught, fatigued, she wanders in the air,

Then as a whirlwind quivers to the ground,

And soon her leaden wing succumbs forlorn,

Her timid cries yet wending through the vales,—

Hark! hark! she calls on Love to hasten home,

To haste, e'en through the illimitable air.

But Silence reigns alone, where Joy once lived,

And on some ancient cliff, pointing to Heaven,

She ever waits (clad in undying grief)

To see his shadow on her mountain-walls.

Thus my true love will mourn dear shattered joys

Which angry storms have late so roughly rent,

And wait to hear the tones of one sweet voice,

Which seem to come from Heaven's ethereal heights,

With silver sweetness falling o'er the heart,

In gentle tenderness, as pleasing Spring.

E'en near the rugged cairn that voice is heard,

By mountain-top, or by the ribbéd sand,

To lead the rolling sea's long moaning chant,

Or like the flutter of the sea-bird laving,

Borne on the ruffled crest of swelling waves.

Those ceaseless waves in wild fantastic shapes

Which bay the moon, reflecting her pale face,—

The bright stars glittering o'er the wide expanse,—

Revive sweet Hope to Love's imaginings!

In midst of such incarnate things Love lives.

In sorrow oft, o'erwhelméd oft, inspired,

Part of the earth, part of high Heaven I seem,

Ever most happy when in deepest thought.

But Love is patient now, and sighs alone:

In midnight's hours these weary eyes unclose,

Just when the screech-owl on the battlement

Talks to her young in fond garrulity;

Or when the moon is riding near a cloud,

As love oft walks in the sequestered grove;

Just when the tired serf is steeped in sleep,

And life's young innocence recounts its grief

In strong entanglements of wandering dreams,

'T is then my woe is so unyielding too,

And will be nursed, whilst many a brazen tongue

In distant towers hastes on the froward day.

As shadows pass and repass, bright, but wan,

I strive to find forgetfulness awhile,

And as a child I count myself to sleep.

Sometimes I hear a rustling as of forms—

Whispering some dream, yet soft and sweet

As the dull wail of Autumn's evening breath,

In dying cadence low, to lull old Time,

And charm the ear with melancholy airs

Which woo to solemn languishment the soul,

Waking the dear and distant scenes now past.

Then Memory breaks in and robs poor Woe

Of Nature's food—the seeming death, soft sleep.

Then fear and strange imaginings arise,

And with such trances blest I seem to see

My Love, arrayed bright as the Morning Star;

Though soon—alas, how soon!—he hastes away,

(As some far-distant sail awakes bright hope,

Then sinks for ever in the far-off waves,)

Too good, too noble, and too pure for Time.

Yet still my Prince remains in Memory's Court,

Amidst a thousand things of mystery,

Veiled in a silvery cloud, so bright and pure,

Encircled o'er with beams of glowing light,

As when soft Summer's morning ray appears.

Such was my treasure—he for whom I sigh,

With whom in sweet communion I dwell,

Waiting awhile amidst the shades of Time,

Whilst its slow step performs its varied works.

And when my soul hath mounted up to God,

In the great kingdom of eternal rest,

Beyond the earth's dark bars and lonely ways,

Its gloom, its gleams of calmness, and its strife,

And all its hurrying tide of present things,

I 'll tell my Love, and all the Angels there,

There lived on earth one cheerful as the lark

In Summer's morn ascending up to Heaven;

But sorrows made her sorrowful exceeding;

And when the evening shadows lengthened far,

And some too careless voice rebuked so loud

The speechless misery of the lonely heart,

Then many recollections weighed her down

So low, so silent, and, alas! forlorn.

I 've heard that Angels watch the long, long night,

With soundless tread their visitations hold,

And speak with voice so soft, and even smile,

Where breaking hearts were drooping very low;

So my poor love will never, never cease,

But Angels tend the throne of its eternity;

Its sighs ne'er die; the past shall ne'er decay,

But bear the freshness of the present hour;

Its dreams are semblance of reality,

And from the font of Memory's bright stream

I live again those hours too quickly past.

Undying love! I hold thee to my heart!

And there are dreams—the dowry of poor grief—

In which I live and walk through all time past,

In sleep's beatitudes and visions decked.

Yes, then from Scotia's rugged happy land

I feel her breezes fan my feverish brow,

Fresh and ambrosial, most definite,

(More real than anything around me now,)

As when the beakéd rock gave shelter safe

From blinding sleet and rapid pelting hail;

Or when amidst the waving fern we sat,

Where varied hues on mound and glen beamed forth,

And grove and vale, with thousand beauties rife,

Suffused with many a ray from Heaven's great towers,

Made Beauty blush with Love's ethereal beams ;

All interspersed the glittering streams ran down,

Like dreamy music revelling everywhere

Around the craggy world of ponderous rocks,

As mirrors for the pallid Queen of Night

When she walks forth from Heaven's high palaces,

With graceful step, to praise the God of Life.

I felt that youthful freshness wafting by,

Which wanders through those ever-verdant vales,

With echo chasing echo round the hills,

And songs came riding on the fragrant wind,

As some sweet spirit's song, melodious,

With sounds celestial as the Almighty's voice.

Awhile the air seemed resting on the breast

Of Silence in her royal manse on earth,

Save ever and anon the low of distant herds

Came through the rustling corn and myriad flowers.

The golden buzzing bee sang, booming forth,

Through streets wrought out with gold and silver spires;

O'er many a leafy bough bright crystals hung;

And flocks in groups went moodily along;

The spider's woof with silver dew all clad;

Fair Nature throbbed in Beauty's tender arms;

So soft the streams did flow, all bright in Heaven.

Ah! then beneath the waning moon we sighed,

And then we prayed. No more. Sweet memory!

Oh! come again, dear transient happiness,

And let me see the tall trees swaying wild,

And watch the painted heather wave so free,

And give me back the visions of the past.

Second Reverie.

REVELATION xiv. 13.

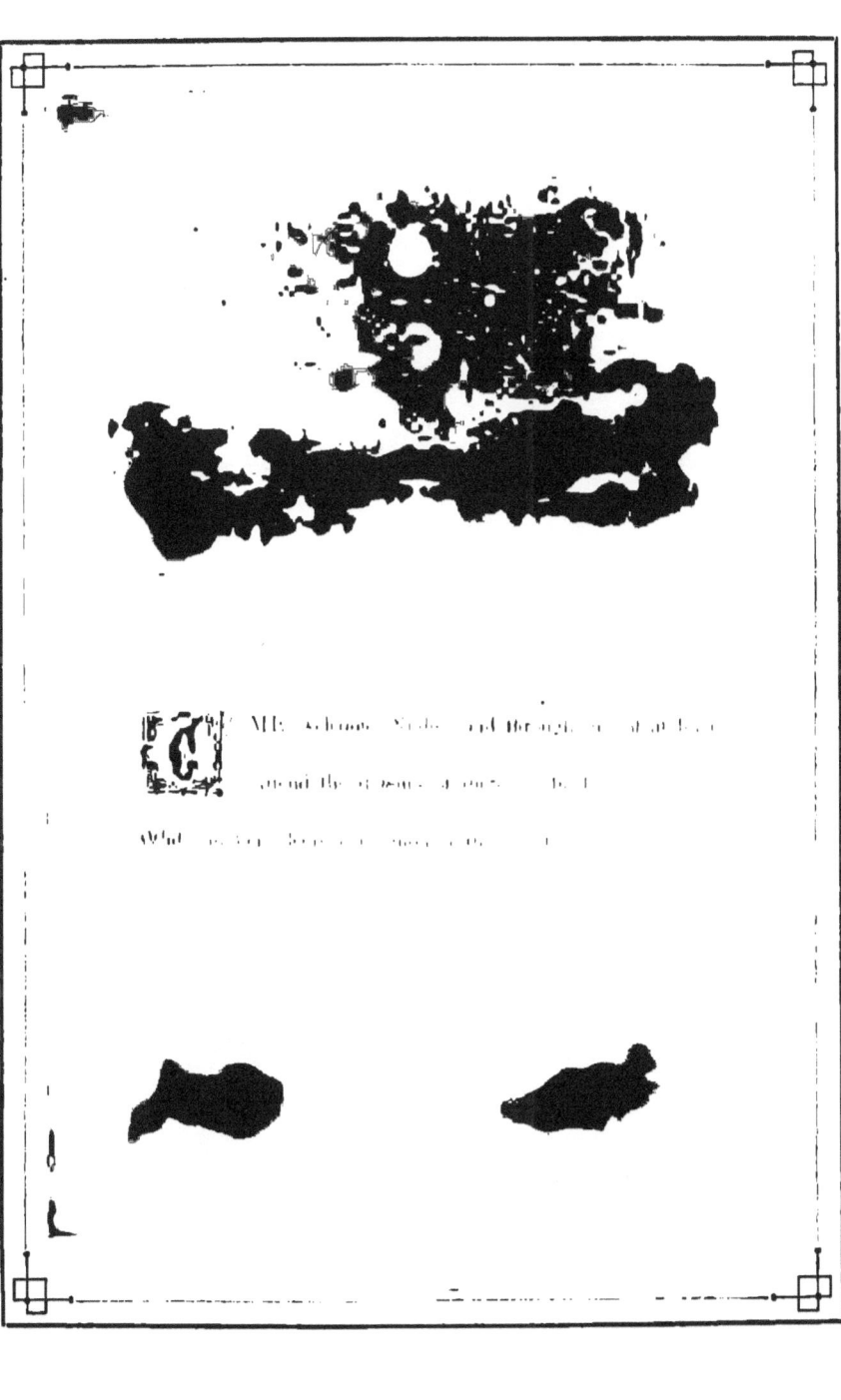

Rides the pale Moon in graceful altitude.

Bright Queen on high! unloose those glittering rays,

To show the path for lonely Sorrow's step,

Whilst musing o'er the faded things of Time,

And all the glimmering past and bygone world,

With many a thought too dear and loved to part.

'Tis sweet to muse in Melancholy's path,

Just when the Moon climbs up the far-off sky,

Leading the clouds to take their silent way,

And listen to the little plaintive dove,

Who tells how sad it is to be alone.

Then, free from curious eye, low in some vale,

Where Love may even dare to count its woes,

And glance e'en to the lofty worlds on high,

And court the brilliant things that gem the sky :

Some, fixed and faithful, watch with anxious eye ;

Some, missive, dart o'er Heaven's sublime expanse,

And cast aside the thin and changing clouds

Which veil the path of Heaven's majestic Queen,

Whose calm and ever-peaceful, holy face

(Seen, through the mist and shadow of the night,

'Midst pine trees dark and high,) serenely glows,

Waiting with courteous mien the early dawn,

Whilst watching all the wanton ways of Time.

Ah ! how unlike the pensive saddened one

Who prays and loves, yet often fears to love

Aught of this earth (so quickly passing on) :

These things must rest with Sorrow and myself.

There is a world! there's mercy ever there,

Which will not break the bruiséd reed. 'T is there

Contrition's prayer is ever heard. 'T is there

That Pride must humbly bow. 'T is there

All transient love, all transient sighs depart.

There Seraphs stand, and in the midst are those

Who out of dark temptation came. Kind Heaven

Will lull the tumults of the aching heart,

That else must burst. The golden gates of Heaven!

To enter there, in faithful penitence,

All earthly comfort, pleasure, state, and power—

Yes! everything below—I'd sacrifice.

My Prince's love is treasured high in Heaven:

This gem I can retain, for ever mine;

Yet I would pray for faith and holiness,

That nothing in this world should stain my soul;

For a divided heart ne'er entered Heaven,—

In that pure world where none may dare to dwell

With whom one sigh, one earthly sigh, remains.

Yet, if the Indian of the torrid climes

Were driven amidst the cold and gloomy bergs

Of icy lands where only strangers dwell,

And, weary with his woe, sank into dreams—

And in the darkness of the night awoke

Quivering with clammy chills and deadly rheums—

Shall he feel joy that all the soothing winds,

And all those cheering rays which on his brow

Oft played in pastime through his perfumed vales.

Are gone?—the noble steed—tiara bright—

And bearings wrought with pearls and glittering gold,

Pure from the bottom of the lonely sea,—

All gone—all fled! The lute's endearing sounds,

In silence steeped, its sweetness heard no more!

When all he loved has left him, and alone,

Shall he rejoice and shout in noisy praise —

Make merriment with strange and chilly forms,

Which thrust aside the kindred things he loves?

Ah, no! his heart low sinks in dreariness,

And for a time he peers with aching eye

And ashy mien; then, glancing pensively,

He just surveys the changes Time has made,

And on his suppliant knee he gently bends;

His weary lids then close 'midst freezing airs;

He smiles, and bows before the gods of home,

And promises afresh his vows to keep.

Suffused in tears of joy, again reclines

In ecstasy, but soon he wakes to grief:

Tear follows tear; he seems to pray to die,

And, starting at the phantom of his home,

He sinks in silence—sinks without a moan,

And all he loved in this great world is gone.

Alas! this angry world oft chides poor Love!

The purest joy which roams from nerve to nerve,

Through every mystic portal, to the brain.

Strange, infinite! Thou holy, heavenly beam,

Which glorifies Affection's first wild dream,

Sweet flower of Time, e'en thou must also die,

But rise again to bloom eternally.

O Love! sweet dream, by Angels shared above,—

Part of that stream which flows direct from Heaven,—

O Love! exalting Love, an Angel thou!

But in deep griefs thy loveliness most seen;

As a bold diver knows the white pearl's bed,

Whilst they who buy and sell this precious thing

Know nothing of her silent beauteous cell.

Love will exalt, although dependence comes,

And forms its nature and its dignity;

As ivy, o'er the ancient turret high,

Clings to the rugged wall; and, whilst it yields,

It borrows strength from might and majesty;

And with its emerald cloak in sombre guise

It decks the noble pile of mother earth,

Diverts the sultry Sun ; and every storm

And hurricane but strengthens its embrace.

Third Reverie.

PSALM xlvi. 1.

 WAS in dull Winter's hours this heart was rent,

When torrents wild, aroused by roaring winds,

Burst from the chambers where the lightning leaps,

 D.

And where the sleeping tempests ever wait,

Whilst Evening's mists and Morning's world of dews

Rush through the mead and by the gentle vale,

Near the green willow and the hazel copse.

Since then the dusky shadow of that woe

Hangs like a heavy cloud, eclipsing all.

The golden vision of my life is gone :

And yet there is a mighty tender Hand,

That guides the down of e'en the thistle's flower,

Which storms have driven recklessly away ;

Then oft the tears of Heaven fall gently forth,

And many a fading flower revives again

Just when the sunbeam hides its golden ray :

And on this everlasting Love I trust,

In certain hope to meet my Prince again.

Till then, sleep on, thou noble form of Time!

Angels will guard thy head; they sing

" Worthy the Lamb, who led the way to Heaven."

The time now past is but a tale part told,

The dulcet dream of earth, but all is gone!

The passing dream with thoughts—impassioned thoughts,

Which gentle souls reciprocate for aye.

Ah, yes! 't is sad, this treacherous world of Time

Has, in its vaunting wantonness, beguiled

A noble Prince to stay awhile on earth,

To march with gallant step o'er its fair face,

To dwell in confidence on passing joys,

The minister of Wisdom's treasury—

Of thought developed by the human mind,

Of soft expressions that the breast inspires,

The wide expansion of the free-born soul,

The concentration of true mental life ;

In love beneficent to all mankind ;

The monitor of nations yet unborn ;

The prop of woman in her earthly path—

Her resting-place, where oft inclined true Love

To tell its joyfulness and all its woes.

He was my guardian and my refuge oft ;

He made me fearless of the world of Time,

And ever thoughtful of the world to come.

The day was ne'er too long—no sorrow then !

And when the evetide hour sank into night,

All seemed a world of peace unspeakable,

Too calm for poor mortality.—I yield

With heart bowed down; I seem shut out from Time.

Alone! ye Angels, listen to that word:

'T is now that world in which my heart succumbs;

Its vastness and interminable depths

Seem ever heaving round my waiting soul.

Then gaze not closely o'er pale Sorrow's face,

For heavy shadows often linger there.

Yes; grief, though under canopies of gold,

Is sometimes lulled to take a kind repose

'Midst perfumes sweet which soothe its weariness.

Alas! there is a woe which never rests,

And there are eyes so full of burning tears,

Which in sad petulance refuse to sleep,

And all night long they seem to love to weep.

O ye who gently walk on Love's soft path,

Say, could ye bear such heavy woe as mine,—

Alone, amidst e'en thousands, yet alone?

'T was such a night as this, in twilight hour,

My Prince and I would loiter in the woods,

Midst rocky heights of Scotia's beauteous land,

Whilst he, with meditating eye, would 'count

Past joys to one who loved to hear that voice,

Telling again the tale of our first love,

Which filled the heart with many happy thoughts.

But now, all gone, on light ethereal wing,

High up in Heaven's great palaces!

Yes, there the soul, from every sorrow free,

In full development, triumphant roams

Through all celestial heights and baseless depths

Of knowledge spiritual and infinite,

Where timid faith yields place to certainty,

And hope is whelmed and lost in constant love.

The brightest Seraphim will lead his step,

And spirits guard his head : my Love now rests

Happy in Heaven ; in safety there he dwells

Where flowers bloom and beauty never fades.

'T is there the just and those we loved on earth

Await—entranced with revelations grand :

There Death succumbs, his crown is there cast down ;

Whilst Love in majesty, eternal Love,

Will there appear with beauteous Charity

In silver sandals bright and pearly robe;

The great Remembrance Book will there be oped,

When God before assembled worlds appears

In great assize to count His jewels forth.

Till then there is a long continuous sleep

Ordained by Love to wait the rest of Time,

Until the choicest herald wakes the good.

Then Death shall abject stand, alone and pale;

Then mortal immortality puts on;

There mighty Death then ends—great end!

Dear, noble Prince, forgive these heaving sighs.

Happy the weary soul which rests like thine!

Thy gentle breath, now hushed, no sighs betray,

All teeming thought and human ecstasy

Hurled down for ever from their tottering thrones,

And all the lights of mind are gone awhile!

Now Fancy's world of dizzy dreams is o'er,

Dispersed in strange dismay so suddenly,—

That ever-genial brow no longer warm,

Though once as radiant as the early morn,

Those noble eyes their wonted ways decline,

Whilst o'er those lids now many a shadow falls,

As evetide shades usurp bright beams of day.

Alas! how long we muse o'er paths of woe!

And down their shadowy vista gaze and sigh.

Dear lord, accept Affection's sacred tear;

Deep in my woes thy beauteous image rests.

Would that this crown and all the things I own

Could purchase back that precious breath of thine !

Yet we shall meet in heavenly climes above,

When rolling years have ta'en their destined way.

For far within the soul are kindred strings,

Which howsoe'er the finger of wild Time

May rudely break, yet Seraphs' hands shall bind

And gather in again, and bid them join

In Love's own symphonies on heavenly harps.

The lustre of those orbs now veiled in Heaven,

The pastime of mortality now gone;

The fount of thine enchanting eloquence

Will ne'er be oped again, until that day

When Heaven shall send its choicest Minister

To roll away the stone which wakeful guards

Shall want the power to stay.   Oh, happy day !

And until then we part, beloved Shade !

Ambitious Death has ta'en my choicest joy !

The beautiful, the virtuous, he seizes first—

All that the heart holds dear, the mind respects.

Yet there are spirits in the vaulted sky,

Beyond the stations of the evening stars,

Who hear the sighs and mark the clouds of Time.

Perchance my Prince may yet delight my ear

With the known accents of his tender voice !

List ! list ! hush !—No, it was the streamlet's voice !

'T is nought—'t is but the wayward sound

Of some dark-foliaged tree, whose arms are moved

By evening's fitful breeze, frighting my soul.

Ye streams! I pray, your rippling murmurs hush;

Ye trembling leaves! now stay your dalliance

With the gay wanton winds; and Nature all

Be mute, lest I should lose the melody

So dear to me. Enchanting sound! Alas!

What passes gently through my listening ear?

Is it sweet echo of his noble voice?

Yet why, alas! should I disturb that peace

With earthly sighs that have no power to save?

Thine is a state too pure for mortal love:

Yet do I pray to whisper in thine ear

Some things of import great. Alas! alas!

Art thou content, good Prince, in this dire dream,

Departing from this verdant world so long?

Say, shall the season which revives the hills

In Spring's bright hour, when flowers first deck the vale,

Arouse thee from this deep and heavy sleep,

Melting the frozen chains which hold those limbs?

Has the supernal world thy parole ta'en,

And may'st thou listen e'en to mortal lips?

Or are there laws inviolable whence thou cam'st,

Which consecrate thy presence in this world?

Doubt not, dear Prince, thy faithful Queen is near,

In sadness wrapt, by sudden storms borne down,

As some pale flower by angry winds laid low.

But stay! perhaps this is a world of dreams,

Which cast sweet life in death, and death in life?

Perhaps I shall awake to joy again.

I dreamt he left his couch while visions strange

Did play their antics on my sleeping mind,

Ere e'en the lid of Morn had 'gan to ope.

Yes, I did dream my Love was wan and sad,

Involved in phantoms strange and varied oft,

Whilst hectic flushes played upon his brow;

But ever and anon some busy thought

In radiance lived, e'en in its slow decline;

And yet around him rushed cold Winter's winds,

And snow's white hoar, as seen on mountain peaks.

Oh! I would dream again—for ever dream,

Nor care again to see the golden Sun,

Which, like a blazing globe of sulph'rous fire,

Betrays my loneliness and mocks my dreams.

Hark! hark! I hear the lark's rejoicing voice,

With mission from this darkened world to Heaven.

The pearly lustre of the Moon is gone,

And gallant day is come, heedless of me.

Now o'er my eyelids wave the wings of light,

Yet visions hover in their viewless path.

O Darkness! lend thine ebon cloak again,

That I may hide my woes from common ken.

Sweet Spirit, list to this my humble lay:

Love waits all clad in saddest fortune's ills.

I dared to love, but now divorced awhile;

Yet have I tokens that true love sustains,

Though oft the source of love's severest pains;

Whilst I, exposed to Sorrow's wintry day,

Must act a part as players in the play,

Who mourn at home—abroad appearing gay.

Let kind eyes weep for me: my heart will burst;

The more I drink of woe, the more I thirst.

Then what avails to watch the golden Morn,

And all the starry children of the Night?

Or timid Cynthia, in her glory clad,

That happy Queen, amidst her silvery worlds?

What doth it serve though emerald Spring should smile,

With music led to many a halcyon bower?

These scenes, though lovely, solace not my soul.

And what avails to hear soft sylvan song—

The cooing dove, or mavis' cheerful voice,

Or lonely nightingale in leafy shades

Wailing the woes of some poor broken heart,

Once full of happy joys? What doth it serve?

Soon passed the dream of joy and youthfulness,

When Time and I were in our happiness.

The heralds from the spotless souls in Heaven

Came down to whisper love and peace at even,

And things my reason may not comprehend.

Sweet, happy dream! bereft of thee, I mourn.

No lute or harp can now revive the past—

The sunshine of my happiness is gone—

All gone, all gone where Beauty swiftly hastes,

To God's great throne, and left this world to me.

Oh, what has time been, since that heavy day

When beauteous forms came down from Heaven's high

    towers,

In silvery dress, in immaterial frame,

Fluttering awhile, as though intent to stay?

One of the angel choir rushed through the air,

Bearing the spirit of my Love away!

And thus my mournful aspect is disclosed.

O gentle Star! I wish that I, like thee,

Could live amongst the clouds, so near to Heaven,

And breathe that mystic air eternally—

Which to the just is given:

Then might I see my Prince all gloriously,

In duteous love, obedient to the cares

Of that estate—so suddenly endowed—

Which to the just is given.

I picture to my mind his heavenly mien—

His gentleness—when missive Angels smile;

The light which hovers round that glorious form—

Which to the just is given.

But why, poor heart! why sink so sad and low?

Time hastens on; I shall depart with joy,

Led by some gentle Angel sent from Heaven,

Bending my course up to that holy clime—

Which to the just is given.

A generous spirit whispers to my heart,

And bids me rest in hope: once more repose,

My trembling soul, and take of love that share—

Which to the just is given.

Say, who can mould the coinage of the brain,

Or phrensy's flight in Evening's stilly hour?

None but the Sacred Guest—the Immortal Friend—

Which to the just is given.

O spring of all my earliest joys!

Drawn from Immanuel's veins, oh, guide these tears

To that pure ever-running stream—

Which to the just is given.

Ah, why look back? for all is gone before,

In safety landed, where no sin

Or shadows darken that bright shore—

Which to the just is given.

When Time is o'er, then come the heavenly hosts,

On wings of gold, in rays of holy light,

To summon forth the long and happy day—

Which to the just is given.

Then shall the Saints land on their native shore,

And those who out of tribulation came,

And all the heavy-laden take that rest—

Which to the just is given.

Yes, soon the nearer waters roll o'er all,

And seraphs' hands shall wipe away all tears,

And lull the cries of loneliness.

Then some poor bosom, which has heaved so long,

Shall heave no more, but ever, ever rest,

And gently lean upon the Saviour's arm!

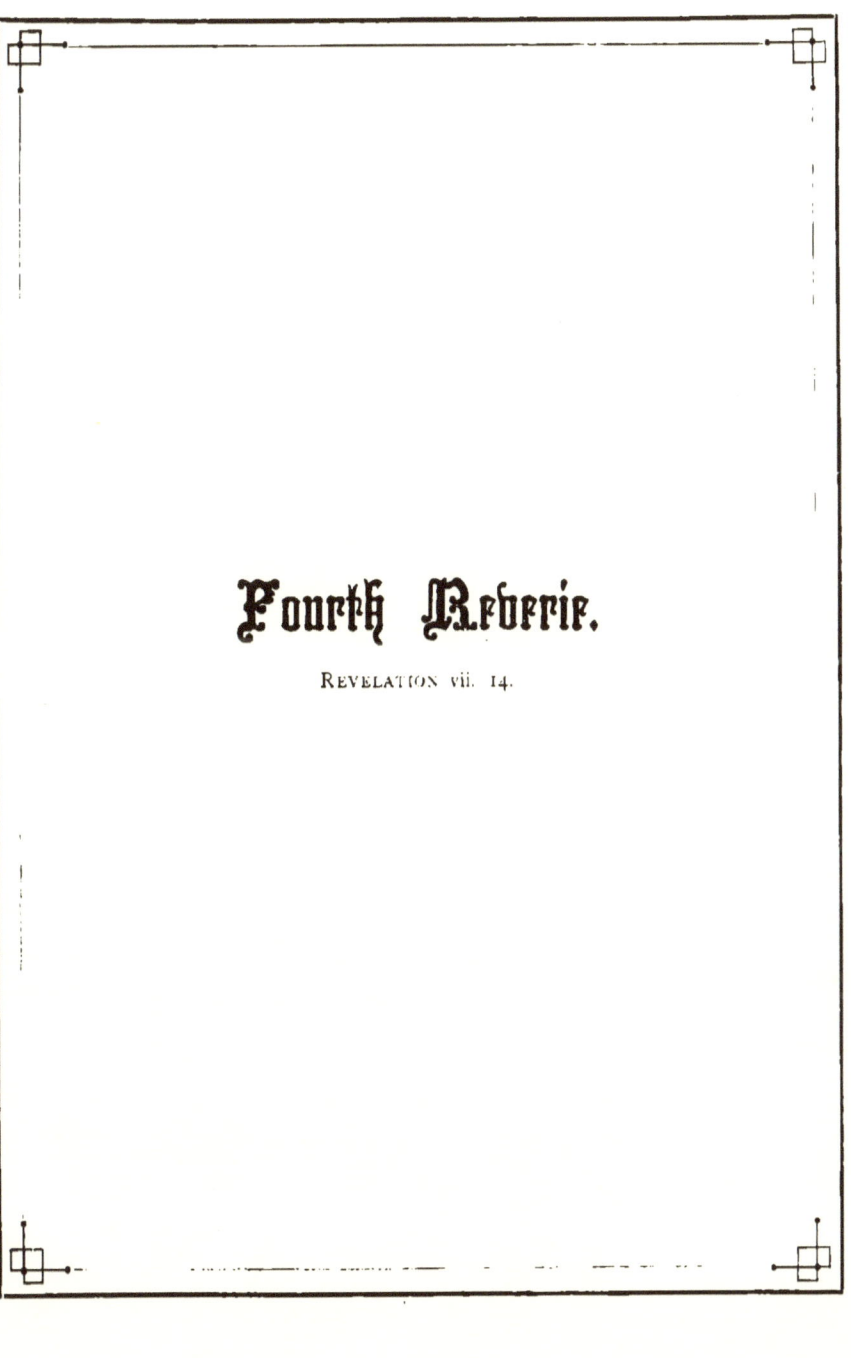

Fourth Reverie.

REVELATION vii. 14.

THE clustering briar leans in wild distraught

Where once the scented bay outspread its leaves;

So soon, all tattered, broken by the storm,

Lies scattered near the bowers where ardent Love,

With tender tumult charged, suffused the soul.

The harp, so late in tune to Love's fond tale,

Has burst its strings in anguish for mine own.

The honeysuckle hides in alcove dense,

From common ken, in light umbrageous folds,

Where oft in pleasing converse Love's kind voice

Would tell Affection's hopes and promises.

Then Time rushed past on silvery wing too quick ;

But now, with heavy gait, he stays with Woe,

To watch pale Sorrow on her wanderings.

I fear, blest Shade, these ever-falling tears

May e'en be grievous to thy new estate,

And I would smile throughout the heavy storm,

And beam as sunshine under darkest clouds;

Yet all my dreams, my waking hours, forbid.

Reproach me not; my heart has borne much woe.

Ask Love to cease to sigh? and ask the Sea

To yield its awful power in tiny drops?

Yes! ask that vaulting Sea to stay awhile?

List to the answer wild:—"Without, within

I am a grave, as Hades deep and dark,

And thus I swallow in my angry jaws

The great, the beautiful, the wise, the good—

The bridal blush in maiden innocence—

The prayer of kindred, winged for sacred home—

The conqueror's triumph, and the captive's groan—

Grieved, unrequited Merit's stifled sigh–

The elbowing insolence of conscious Wealth—

The gold of Ophir and the chains of slaves—

The bartered smile—the transient bliss—

In me, with vile corrupting things, unseen

They lie,—whilst I roll on my lonely way.

'T is thus I grind out of these mortal hearts

The direst veneration dust can yield.

'T is thus I make them bow in humid death,

And cast their boasted honours at my feet."

Just so is Sorrow slow to hear the wise,

And clings enamoured to its dreariness,

Yet prays and waits, and fears 'mid timid hope.

Ah! never, never chide my restless woe;

To grieve for love is my rich destiny.

Who dares to vaunt or count the sighs of love?

Go to the Sea, and from its sandy mount

Count one by one—and ever, ever count.

Alas! this heart now deeply moans and heaves

Heavily, as oft the vexed and angry deep

Will throw its ancient firm foundations in the air,

And scatter all its dusky atoms wide,

Which in past time, with golden sands below,

Would sparkle with the countless riches there.

One weary night I dreamt great angry waves

Came surging, rolling, heaving after me:

E'en to the bottom of the sullen Sea

They urged me down triumphantly.

I thought how sad and dreadful 'twas to be

With all the awful things in silence there!

I heard a voice as of a thousand sounds!

I looked upon the far-off, trembling Sea,

And saw the Cross my Saviour bore,—

Whence beams of beauteous light betrayed the graves

Where lie the myriads of the long-since dead:

Some, once like me, so suddenly bereft,

Or torn from happy life.

                              But what is life?

'T is but a visionary span—

So quickly gone.   How brief that little span!

As some poor fragment from the heaving hulk,

Torn by some struggling, trembling hand,

Drifting along the haughty boiling sea,

Which wallows joyously,

And draws its victim to the depths below,

Soon dashed and shattered like a tiny shell,

Where surf and swell in angry waves break round,

And wake the sea-bird in her airy nest,—

There lie the beautiful and good for aye,

Where gleaming aisles are sculptured by the waves.

Thus suddenly my heart's best treasure sank!

But peaceful death will come, absorbing all;

And then the Resurrection morn—when Heaven

Will give me back that Pearl, which being lost,

Leaves me a timid bankrupt and alone.

But He who rules the heavens, the earth, the sea,

And before whom all Potentates must stand,

Has called away my treasure for awhile.

Hark! hark! I hear some Angel's silver voice—

"He shall return, though now to mortal sight

The loveliest rose on earth is veiled awhile;

Though now the passing clouds delay the light,

Yet it but sleeps as beam in Sorrow's tear."

Hush, ye rude, wandering winds, and lightly blow,

In soft and dying cadence! bear your wings

To your far-distant homes, where southern skies

Shed brighter beams upon the smiling earth.

Go!—go, where cascades clear and crystal streams

Did erst suppress their murmur sweet, to list

The sweeter sounds, with which the Mantuan reed

All vocal made the sunny vine-clad hills

And orange bowers, so loved in days bygone.

'T is well, all well—this earth must pass away,

With all the shadowy things of this cold world,

Its hopes and fears.   Then will descend from Heaven

The fairest, meekest of the spiritual world,

The herald, Mercy, smiling through her tears.

Yes—yes ! she's pointing to the spotless robe,

All love.   And then those stars and changeful moon

Must sink within those far unknown degrees

Which the great King of Heaven did first conceive.

Then shall renew the sweet embrace of love,

Which shall for ever and for ever be :

But that tall castle height must lowly bend ;

The mountain where the golden sun has hid ;

Those rocks where lonely eagles find their rest;

The peaceful valley where the kine oft lowed;

The boundaries of the raging billows' crest;

The Pleiades and wild Arcturus too,

Must render up their native majesty

When the archangel's final trumpet sounds,

Which calls the varied tribes of men to Heaven.

But Love's exhaustless song, all melody,

Shall lead the choirs of Heaven's great palaces,

And, in the presence of Almighty Love,

Shall sound his sweetest notes for ever there.

But stay, lone Sorrow, stay! all of this earth must change.

When sun, and moon, and every glistening star

Shall have their greatest exercise performed,

And life is whelmed in immortality,

Then, quick as morning sun, with orient beams,

Shall wake the waiting spirits of the dead,

And moving myriads fill that solemn vale,

Soon to arise 'midst burning lustrous light,

In troops to meet the Saviour in the skies.

Some near the pathless ocean slowly wend,

Or down the craggy mountain, decked with snow;

Some resting, stop as tired winds from storms;

Some vault 'midst fleecy clouds which buoyant ride,

Or congregate and muse of worlds above:

In solemn troops, through mystic airs, they move.

So shall my Love, with holy glory clad,

Arise with saints no eye hath ever seen,

With timid glance, and step of heavenly mien.

From opening clouds shall varied spirits come,

From mountain's side, from all the paths of Time,

Where joy, or hope, or love has ever been,

And all from sad temptation's angry fire

Shall rise, from mouldering dust and Death's attire;

The beings of the present, of the past, shall come—

The long-since dead, forgotten or forlorn—

The Prince who lived enthroned in Sorrow's heart,

And those bedecked with many a jewelled crown—

The peasant, long remembered in his home—

The gentle fair one hurried to the tomb—

In wide assembly shall at once resort

Men of true fame, beloved in days bygone.

The faithful one, the Widow left alone—

With all the tenderest ties which earth may know,

Shall bloom afresh, and ever, ever grow.

They shall arise, led by the Saviour's hand,

To join the grand assemblage of the just.

There, free from passion and delusive hope,

Or death, or change, or fear, or strife, or woe,

A better, higher, dearer love be theirs.

A bright, ne'er-fading light shall ever burn,

Which, by the mystic hands of angels fed,

Will shine whilst countless years shall ever roll.

The Rock of Ages then their surest stay,

No more on giddy height or slippery way.

No more shall courtiers gorgeously pass by,

No more the singers may seduce the ear,

Or meaner fashion dissipate the eye;

But with firm foot upon the world, the flesh,

And all the tyranny of Time and things,

Free from the magic arts of demons' rage,

They shall arise and walk, with stately step,

Where the archangels tend with glittering wings.

On many a slope illumed by Heaven's great light,

They sit in groups and attitudes serene,

To tell their varied tale of nether life,

And hear the secret of the King of kings.

Then, looking to the Cross, see there unveiled

Eternal recompense for every woe.

Behold, the bow of Heaven embrightens now,

And dare I join the radiancy once more?

Yet have I fear! I would be just to all;

But if some storm should break the barriers,

And on some eve wild wanderings once more

Should sound like woe in penitential mood,

And should this heart e'en tremble very low,

(As oft the aspen quivers in the vale,)

And fall again into drear reverie,

Be sure I'll stay the current of the tears,

(Which might assuage the burning heat within,)

And find some gladless home for gentle Grief;

Yet the last trembling sound of true love's tongue

Will be for him, the "noble and the good."

Yet I will try to sigh no more—no more!

Yes, I will check the oft-reviving tear,

And dedicate dear Memory to Heaven,

Whilst round me shine the children of my Love,

And in the sunshine of the present times

Live high enthroned in hearts for ever mine.

VISITATION OF ANGELS.

Visitation of Angels.

OUR readers will perceive that we believe that good and bad angels attend on the devious path of mortality, and wait around the bed whilst sleeping hours roll along. Perhaps we gained this faith from Scripture; though we confess we have always felt, as though by intuition, that we could leave some anxieties to some shadow of ourselves, or some protector or herald whom we could not see, but with whom we were ever ready to make bargain and contract as to sins and fallings-off from vows. Ah, reader! the world may be learned in many things, and know our stature, and make nice calculations and comparisons concerning our virtue and character, talents and physical constitution; but who can follow the fairy step, or hear the mystic voice, or see the golden halo of our good angel? or collect the Circean whisperings of our bad angel, or hear the awful, yet majestic, thundering of his trident when he fails to win our spirits, or we refuse to drink from the intoxicating bowl he bears, in which Death lies lurking?

We know that some will smile whilst we talk thus; but we may remind our readers that many of the ancient heathens (probably from tradition) entertained some such notion, that beings of a superior order were ever ministering between men and God. The Greeks termed them "demons" (knowing ones), and the Romans, "genii."

Socrates said, on the day of his death, " My demon gives me notice every morning of an evil which will befall me that day, but did not give me notice of any evil this day, therefore I cannot regard as any evil my being condemned to die." Some have said this demon was his reason; but those who are acquainted with his sayings know that he never spoke in such obscure and ambiguous terms: if he had meant his reason, his integrity and exactness of character would have indicated this precisely.

An ancient poet, who lived several ages before Socrates, speaks more determinately. Hesiod says,

" Millions of spiritual creatures walk the earth unseen.

Hence, it is probable, arose the tales about the exploits of
their demigods *(minorum gentium)*, their satyrs, fauns, and
nymphs of every kind, wherewith they supposed both sea
and land to be filled. These are, like the age, dark and
unsatisfactory evidences, standing alone, and producing no
faith or conclusions.

God only knows, and has revealed in our spirits and by
His revelation, all which is needful. Saint Paul says, in
Hebrews i. 14, " Are they not all ministering spirits, sent
forth to minister unto them that shall be heirs of salvation ?"
and the Psalmist says, " Who maketh His angels spirits, and
His ministers a flame of fire " (civ. 4). We are told, " They
sang together when the foundations of the earth were laid."

Dr. Parnell makes the angel say to the hermit, concerning the death of a child,

> "To all but thee in fits he seemed to go,
> And 't was my ministry to deal the blow."

Marcus Antoninus, a heathen, a philosopher, and an emperor, in his Meditations says, "I thank God for revealing to me, when I was at Cajeta, in a dream, what totally cured that disease which none of my physicians were able to heal." We will not add more than our joy that "they are more that are for us than they that are against us ;" and we cannot refrain quoting the words of pious Bishop Ken :

> "Oh, may Thy angels, while I sleep,
> Around my bed their vigils keep ;
> Their love angelical instil ;
> Stop every avenue of ill.

May they celestial joys rehearse,
And thought to thought with me converse."

We have reflected thus concerning angels or spirits; and, although we will not pronounce any absolute opinion concerning the mystery of the Holy Spirit, yet we ourselves have sometimes thought it was as a good angel in our pilgrimage in this strange land; and we will leave the Christian to reflect on the words of our Saviour: "If ye love me, keep my commandments. And I will pray the Father, and He shall give you another Comforter, that He may abide with you for ever; even the Spirit of truth; whom the world cannot receive, because it seeth Him not, neither knoweth Him: but ye know Him, for He dwelleth with you, and shall be in you." (John xiv. 15—17.) We even believe

that Jesus Himself was the Angel who struggled with Jacob;
and, we rejoice to say, we believe that our Holy Advocate,
who is now sitting on the jasper throne (upon whose thigh
is the word Immanuel), is ever sending legions of angels to
enlighten and guide the heirs of the kingdom of heaven;
and through them He again says, " Let not your heart be
troubled, neither let it be afraid. Ye have heard how I said
unto you, I go away, and come again unto you."

We have preferred to talk of good angels; yet truth re-
quires that we should remember the words of the Apostle :
" We wrestle not against flesh and blood, but against prin-
cipalities, against powers, against the rulers of the darkness
of this world, against wicked spirits in heavenly places."
(Ephes. vi. 12.) The great poet (Milton) seems to have

fully believed that each man and woman had good and bad angels. The eloquent Gessner makes an evil angel (Anamalech) cast himself at full length by the dead body of the amiable Abel, and exultingly say, "Rise, beautiful youth! rise, thou friend of angels! this indolence in thy orisons ill becomes the worship of thy God! But he stirs not. His own brother hath left him weltering in his blood. No; that honour is mine: I guided the arm of the fratricide." And then he reflects upon returning to hell, and giving an account of his mission: "I shall rise above the vile populace of hell. I hasten to the foot of the infernal throne. The vast concave of the fiery gulf will reverberate my praises." In Genesis xvi. 7: "And the angel of the Lord found her [Hagar] by a fountain of water in the wilderness,

by the fountain in the way to Shur." Also in verse 10,
" The angel of the Lord said unto her, I will greatly multiply
thy seed," etc.

The word *angel* appears in many parts of Scripture. The
Greek word *angelos* and the Hebrew *melach* are both words
denoting messenger. The term is used very indefinitely in
Scripture ; sometimes the Deity Himself, His providence,
and the impersonal agents of His will—sometimes the pro-
phets and holy men : it is also extended to the ministers and
agents of the devil. The Rabbins and Fathers have written
elaborately on this head ; but enough appears in the Scrip-
tures for true knowledge.

The Jews, as well as the early Christians, seemed to have
believed that good and bad angels attended every one.

Rhoda says (when hearing the voice of Peter), "It is his angel." After all we have said, let us remember that there is a chief to all the evil angels,—

> "A constant watch he keeps,
> He eyes us night and day;
> He never slumbers, never sleeps,
> Lest he should lose his prey."

And we must take our share of the inheritance ; for the Saviour of the world was tempted even unto the last; and let us be also able to say, "Father, into Thy hands I commend my spirit."

On the term δαιμων, Schrevelius, by *Major*, gives the following significations : "a god, spirit, genius, demon, good or bad fortune, chance ; *among the sacred writers*, an unclean spirit, a devil."

Ουδ' επιορκησω πρυς δαιμονος [*by a god*]—*Hom. Il.* xix. 188.

Εστι δ' ανδρι φαμεν
Εοικος αμφι δαιμονων καλα.—*Pindar, Olymp.* stroph. ii. 9.

It is becoming to a man to speak
Honourable things *of the gods.*

Hederic gives the following: "a god, a hero, a genius;

fortune, both good and bad; in the New Testament, a devil."

τις ὁ μηδησας
μειζονα δαιμων των μακιστων
προς ση δυσδαιμονι μοιρα.—*Soph. Œdip. Rex,* 1300.

What demon (is it) that has sprung, with a violence
Greater than the greatest, to thy wretched fate?

ι ω δαιμον, ιν' εξηλλου.—*Soph. Œdip. Rex,* 1311.

O Fortune, to what hast thou tended!

τις σ' επηρε δαιμονων.—*Soph. Œdip. Rex,* 1325.

What god [demon] instigated thee?

94

στυγερος δαιμων [an evil deity].—*Od.* v. 369.

κακος δαιμων [an evil deity].—*Od.* x. 64.

προς δαιμονα [against the divine power].—*Il.* xvii. 98.

συν δαιμονι [with the favour of God].—*Il.* xi. 792.

Æschylus, in the tragedy of the "Persai" (620), calls the

deified Darius δαιμων.

Φευδωνυμως σε δαιμονες Προμηθεα
καλουσιν.—*Æschyli, Prome.* 85.

Prometheus,
The *gods** falsely call you the Provident.

ει τι μη δαιμων παλαιος νυν μεθεστηκε στρατω.—*Æschy.*
Persæ, 154.

Unless our ancient *tutelary genius* has now passed over to the army
[sometimes a *good* or *malevolent spirit*, causing the good or ill fortune of
men].

---

* Or, perhaps, demigods (as distinguished from θεοι).

λυσσωντι δ' αυτω δαιμονων δεικνυσι τις.—*Soph. Œd. Rex,*
1158.

Some demon shows (her) to him raving.

που τις θεων,
η δαιμων εστ' επαρωγος.—*Eurip. Hec.* 162.

Where is there any god or *demon*
That will give me aid?

ὁιαν, ὁιαν αυ σοι λωβαν
εχθισταν αρρηταν τ'
ωρσεν τις δαιμων.—*Eurip. Hec.* 200.

What wrong, what (outrage) most hateful and
Unutterable, some demon has aroused against thee?

Our readers remember the innumerable Scripture authorities; and we had intended to extend this note, having
collected many and various authorities, but we fear being
tedious.